Ex-Library: Friends of
Lake County Public Library

Armadillo Tattletale

by helen ketteman · illustrated by keith graves

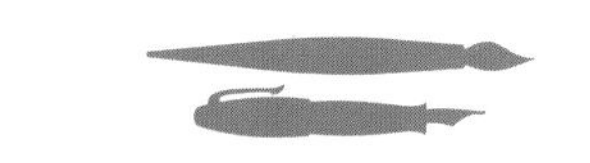

SCHOLASTIC PRESS/NEW YORK

LAKE COUNTY PUBLIC LIBRARY

In the bare bones beginning, Armadillo's ears were as tall as a jackrabbit's and as wide as a steer's horns. With such wonderful ears, Armadillo could hear anything and everything. And he loved nothing better than eavesdropping on other animals and telling tales about what he heard.

But as good as his ears were for hearing, they dragged in the dirt, and stuck in the muck after a rain, and always made him trip. Thus Armadillo was the slowest of creatures.

And since the other animals disliked him for telling tales, they beat him to the watering hole every day and forced Armadillo to scrounge through the mud for a puddle of murky water to drink. It tasted awful and practically made him sick, so he drank as little as possible, and was always thirsty.

One day, as Armadillo stumbled around searching for a puddle, he overheard Egret whisper to Turtle, "Blue Jay's feathers are looking a bit scraggly. I wonder if the poor bird is sick. I'll call on him tomorrow to see if I can be of help."

But Armadillo went to Blue Jay first, twitching his little tail as he spoke. "I heard Egret talking about you," he said in a sing-song voice. "She thinks you're scraggly-looking."

Blue Jay squalled and he bawled, and he squawked and he gawked, and he otherwise threw one humongous hissy fit.

When Egret heard what had happened, she went straightaway to Armadillo. "What you told Blue Jay was not true! Anyway, my words were not for your ears!" she scolded. And she pick-pecked his ears good and proper, and gave him the what-for and the how-come and the why-not.

Armadillo cried great big armadillo tears, and he promised never to tell tales again.

But the next day, while searching the mud for a sip of water, Armadillo heard Muskrat and Butterfly talking, and he hid in the bushes to listen.

"Rattlesnake's rattles used to be terribly out of tune, but now they sound wonderful. She must be taking music lessons," said Muskrat.

Armadillo tripped over to where Rattlesnake lay warming herself in the sun. He shifted his weight from foot to foot in an awkward armadillo dance. Rattlesnake opened an eye, and Armadillo grinned. "I heard Muskrat talking about you. He said your rattles sound terrible and out of tune."

Rattlesnake rattled and she prattled, and she fussed and she cussed, and she otherwise threw one humongous hissy fit.

When Muskrat heard what had happened, he scurried to Armadillo. "You twisted my words into something I did not say!" he shrieked. "Besides, my words were not for your ears!" And he whick-whacked his tail at Armadillo, and gave him the what-for and the how-come and the why-not.

Armadillo cried buckets of tears, and he promised never, ever to tell tales again.

But the next day, while slogging through the mud looking for a drink, Armadillo saw Alligator and Blue Heron talking, and he stepped behind a rock to listen.

“Toad’s skin is looking so much better than it used to. I wonder if she changed her diet,” said Alligator.

Armadillo shuffled off to find Toad. "I heard Alligator say your skin is plug-ugly and you should go on a diet," he said with a twinkle in his eye.

Toad hopped and she flopped, and she wailed and she railed, and she otherwise threw one humongous hissy fit.

When Alligator found out what Armadillo had said, she hurried to find him. "Why did you tell Toad those things? I never said them!" she snapped. "Anyway, my words were not for your ears!" She gave him the what-for and the how-come and the why-not.

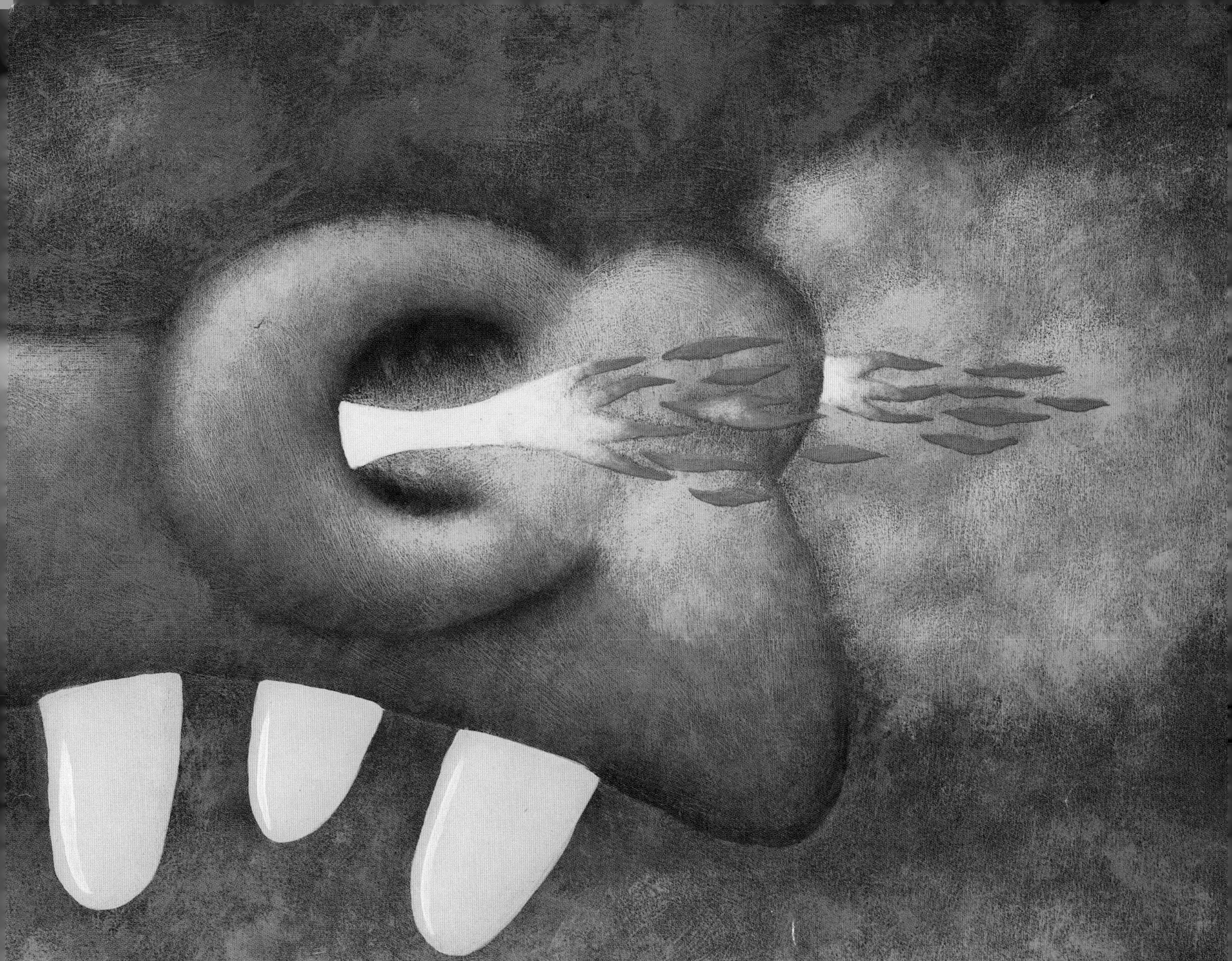

"And now," she said, "I'll fix your ears so you won't be snooping and telling tales again!" And she opened her mouth and gnashed and clashed her big, strong alligator teeth.

And then she nipped and snipped and clipped at Armadillo's ears until there was nothing left but tiny, teeny, itsy, weenie little ears.

When she finished, Armadillo looked at his reflection in a puddle. His ears were so tiny!

Then he started to cry. Oh, did he cry. He raised such a ruckus that all the animals came to see what had happened. When they saw his ears—his new tiny, teeny, itsy, weenie little ears—they stared, and they gawked, and they whispered.

Armadillo stopped crying. "What?" he asked. "What are you whispering?" Everyone gaped at Armadillo because, for the first time, he hadn't quite heard.

"It was not for your ears anyway," Muskrat called out.

Armadillo's faced turned red. "I did not hear the whispers, but I heard that!" he said, chasing after Muskrat. In seconds, Armadillo caught him.

"Did you see how fast Armadillo ran?" Muskrat shouted.

"He didn't trip at all!" added Blue Jay.

"Why, he's so fast, now we'll never be able to keep him away from the fresh water!" said Rattlesnake.

Armadillo felt his tiny, teeny, itsy, weenie little ears. "Fresh water!" he shouted. "That is just what I want! And it's fun to run fast!" Then he danced and raced in circles and zig-zags all the way to the watering hole, where he drank as much fresh, clear water as he wanted. "From now on, I will never be thirsty again!"

And he wasn't.

He also stopped telling tales, for even though he could hear with his tiny, teeny, itsy, weenie little ears, he couldn't overhear the other animals' conversations.

To this day, armadillos have small ears. They always drink their fill of fresh water. And you may hide in the bushes and listen as long as you like, but you will never, ever catch an armadillo telling tales.

3 3113 01990 3311

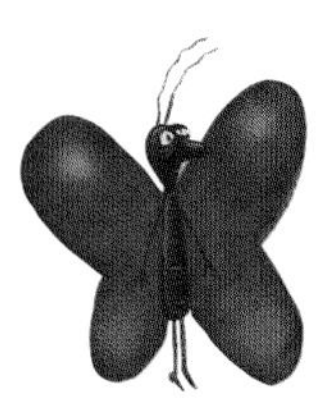

To my wonderful friend Julie Cowan,
with thanks and admiration. Much love,
-H. K.

To Nancy.
-K. G.

Text copyright © 2000 by Helen Ketteman
Illustrations copyright © 2000 by Keith Graves
All rights reserved. Published by Scholastic Press, a division of Scholastic Inc., *Publishers since 1920.* SCHOLASTIC, SCHOLASTIC PRESS and associated logos are trademarks and/or registered trademarks of Scholastic Inc.

No part of this publication may be reproduced, or stored in a retrieval system, or transmitted in any form or by any means, electronic, mechanical, photocopying, recording, or otherwise, without written permission of the publisher. For information regarding permission, write to Scholastic Inc., Attention: Permissions Department, 555 Broadway, New York, NY 10012.
Library of Congress Cataloging-in-Publication Data
Ketteman, Helen.
Armadillo tattletale / by Helen Ketteman;
illustrated by Keith Graves. p. cm.
Summary: Armadillo's habit of eavesdropping and then misreporting what he hears makes the other animals so angry that they find a way to keep him from overhearing their private conversations.
ISBN 0-590-99723-8
[1. Armadillos Fiction. 2. Animals Fiction. 3. Gossip Fiction.]
I. Graves, Keith, ill. II. Title. PZ7.K494Wh 2000 [Fic]-dc21 99-14722 CIP

10 9 8 7 6 5 4 3 2 1 0/0 1 2 3 4

Printed in Mexico 49
First printing, September 2000
The text type was set in 21 point Heatwave.
The illustrations were rendered in acrylic paint, ink, and colored pencil.
Display type hand-lettered by Keith Graves
Book design by Kristina Albertson